THE STRANGER

THE STRANGER

MAPLE SPRING PUBLISHING

Published 2024 by Maple Spring Publishing

Front cover design by David Rheinhardt of Pyrographx
Interior design by Jason Snyder

Library of Congress Cataloging-in-Publication Data is available upon request

ISBN: 979-8-3505-0107-0

10 9 8 7 6 5 4 3 2 1

THE STRANGER

Screenplay by Anthony Veiller
(Orson Welles *and* John Huston *uncredited*)
Adapted by Victor Trivas *and* Decla Dunning
Story by Victor Trivas
Copyright © 1946 · Shooting Script, 1946
RKO Radio Radio Pictures, Inc.

CAST

Orson Welles . . . . . Franz Kindler/Professor Charles Rankin

Edward G. Robinson . . . . Mr. Wilson

Loretta Young. . . . . .Mary Longstreet Rankin

Philip Merivale . . . . Judge Adam Longstreet

Richard Long . . . . Noah Longstreet

Konstantin Shayne. . . . . .Konrad Meinike

Byron Keith .Dr. Jeffrey Lawrence

Billy House . . . . Mr. Potter

Martha Wentworth . . . . .Sara

Isabel O'Madigan . . . . .Mrs. Lawrence

Pietro Sosso. . . . . .Mr. Peabody

Erskine Sanford. . . . . Party Guest

The film begins with a SECRETARY exiting a door with the sign "Allied War Crimes Commission, Dept. 12." She carries some files.

FADE IN:
BLUE SKY—DAY

Close-up of WILSON, with prison gates behind him. He is smoking a pipe. His face is grim as he listens to men's voices off scene.

WILSON

Leave the cell door open, that's all there is to it. Let him escape.

The CAMERA pulls back to reveal several MEMBERS of the War Crimes Commssion.

FIRST VOICE
(an English accent)

In my view, it's all very irregular. It might entail the most embarrassing repercussions—

SECOND VOICE
(French accented)

Exactement. Certainly. It is a responsibility of the first magnitude.

I'm sorry, Mr. Wilson, but you must see . . .

Suddenly, without warning, WILSON turns on them. His voice is sharp with suddenly released rage.

WILSON
Blast all this discussion. What good are words . . .

(gesturing with his pipe)

I'm sick of words . . . Hang the repercussions and the responsibility. If I fail . . . I'm responsible. Leave the cell door open! Let him escape! Let him! It's our only chance! You can threaten me with the bottom pits of hell . . . and still I insist.

(he pounds on the desk for emphasis, the pipe still in his hand)

This obscenity must be destroyed. You hear me? Destroyed!

WILSON slams his pipe down on the table, breaking it.

FADE OUT:

FADE IN:
EXT. DECK—NIGHT (CRANE SHOT)

MEINIKE, in shadow, is walking on the deck of a passenger ship, muttering to himself.

VOICE OF ANNOUNCEMENT
Todos pasajeros disembarcen! All passengers ready to disembark!

MEINIKE
(muttering to himself)

I am traveling for my health . . . I am traveling for my health . . .

MEINIKE turns around; we see WILSON, with his back turned to us, identified by his now repaired pipe, on which he is puffing. MEINIKE does not see him.

VOICE OF ANNOUNCEMENT

Tenga vistas y passaportes! Get your passports ready!

MEINIKE
(muttering to himself)

I am traveling for my health . . .

EXT. LOWER LEVEL OF DOCK SHED—NIGHT

MEINIKE approaches the immigration desk, behind which an IMMIGRATION OFFICIAL and the Ship's PURSER sit side by side. Opposite them are lined up the ship's PASSENGERS. An AMERICAN LADY, MRS. DEVRIES is talking to the OFFICER.

As the OFFICIAL examines the next person, the CAMERA SWINGS SLIGHTLY to focus on MEINIKE, the next in line. His lips move in a soundless rhythm of "I am traveling for my health . . . I am traveling for my health . . ."

MADAME DE VRIES

I'm afraid I don't understand.

OFFICIAL

Your business in this country, Senora?

MADAME DE VRIES

I am joining my husband.

OFFICIAL

(stamping the passport)

Next, please.

MEINIKE shuffles the necessary step forward and extends his passport with trembling fingers; his lips continue to move.

OFFICIAL

(with same casualness as he opens the passport)

Stefan Polowski.

As he pronounces the name, he hands the passport to the PURSER.

PURSER

(looking up at Moinike)

Your business in this country, Señor?

MEINIKE once again completes his silent repetition of the phrase, then speaks it aloud.

MEINIKE

I am traveling for my health.

OFFICIAL

Health?

MEINIKE

I am traveling for my health.

OFFICIAL

Oh. You are a native of what country?

MEINIKE

Poland.

CAMERA CRANES UP to WILSON, standing on the upper level of the dock. He is leaning against a pillar, but we do not see his face; only his pipe. As we watch him, he removes his dead pipe from between his lips and raps the inverted bowl twice against the pillar. SENORA MARVALES is standing next to him. But we do not see their faces. We hear the sound of a passport being stamped and the OFFICIAL's voice.

OFFICIAL'S VOICE
(Over Scene)

Next, please.

SENORA MARVALES descends from the upper deck and follows MEINIKE on the main deck. He continues on, but she turns and goes down a flight of stairs, where a MAN is waiting in a vehicle.

MAN

Que paso?

SENORA MARVALES
(says something in Spanish)

MARVALES

Bien.

He drives off.

STONE BRIDGE—NIGHT SKY

This DISSOLVE is almost a FADE OUT, the CAMERA being focused on the limitless darkness of a night sky.

We see MRS. MARVALES as she follows MEINIKE, who walks across a rustic bridge. There is the sound of a slow, sad tango and the faint murmur of voices. MEINIKE is passing a cheap nightclub.

As MEINIKE moves out of scene, CAMERA remains stationary, still tilted up. MARVALES is standing in the recess of the window, his face half hidden, as he watches MEINIKE in the street below. In his room, MARVALES picks up a phone.

MARVALES
(into phone)

Hotel Nacionale? Siete, siete, cero, dos . . .

We hear the ringing of a telephone.

We see the shadow of a cradle telephone as a hand reaches for it and picks it up. Next to the phone are a couple of books, one open. WILSON's hand closes one. We see its title: The Old Clock Book. Under it is The Clock Book by Wallace Nutting. WILSON's hand sets down his pipe on top of it.

WILSON

Hello? Yes.

(pause)

You haven't lost him? You're sure you know where he's going?

MARVALES—AT WINDOW—NIGHT

MARVALES
(into phone)

My wife is following him; he is going to the photographer's, probably to get a new passport—and new instructions.

DISSOLVE TO:
INT. PHOTOGRAPHER'S STUDIO—
CLOSE SHOT—MEINIKE EARLY DAWN

We see MEINIKE's face in a mirror. The PHOTOGRAPHER, next to the mirror, takes a shot of him.

MEINIKE
(in a loud voice)

I wish to know the whereabouts of Franz Kindler. Franz Kindler.

The PHOTOGRAPHER starts.

PHOTOGRAPHER
(slowly)

There is no Franz Kindler. Franz Kindler is dead . . . and cremated.

MEINIKE comes into the shot, his face shadowed in quarter view.

MEINIKE
(shouting)

It's a command!

(his voice lowers but its intensity remains)

I have a message for Franz Kindler. From the All Highest.

PHOTOGRAPHER
(uncertainly)

It is forbidden.

MEINIKE
(his voice high and piercing)

I command you in the name of that authority!

Invoking this power intimidates the PHOTOGRAPHER. He moves across the shabby room. He pauses at a small table on which there is a large album, then hesitates, glances back at MEINIKE.

The PHOTOGRAPHER begins to leaf through the album, turning pages slowly. He stops, turns to stare at MEINIKE. The PHOTOGRAPHER, with a doubtful sigh, turns a few more pages in the album, and removes a picture postcard.

PHOTOGRAPHER
You know the name he's using?

MEINIKE does not answer but reaches for the card.

*INSERT—CLOSE SHOT—PICTURE
POSTCARD HARPER TOWN SQUARE*

On the postcard is a photograph of the Harper Square: main street, shops, and church. We can see the clock in the church tower, but it is inconspicuous. Written on the bottom of the card are the numerals "23478-678901," and "Harper, Connecticut."

MEINIKE
Con-nec-ti-cut. In the United States. The town of Harper.

FADE IN:
EXT. HARPER CLOCK TOWER—DAY

The scene turns to the main square of Harper. We see the church with the clock tower, identical to the picture on the postcard. CAMERA NOW SWINGS AND PANS DOWN to disclose the Harper town square, fronting a green, around which the township itself is clustered.

A bus pulls up in front of Potter's Drugs. Inside the bus, the DRIVER calls out:

DRIVER

Harper!

MEINIKE gets up to take down his bag. As he does, WILSON is already taking down his own bag. His repaired pipe falls on the floor. WILSON picks it up.

WILSON

Oh. Excuse me.

MEINIKE looks at WILSON with apprehension, then hastily takes his bag and leaves the bus. WILSON takes his bag and follows him.

MEINIKE goes into Potter's Drugstore, looking uneasy.

POTTER is seated at an open window, laughing at a radio broadcast.

WILSON comes up to the window.

POTTER

Good afternoon. Have a nice trip?

WILSON

Yes, thank you.

MEINIKE looks at them both with extreme apprehension.

WILSON

Quite a fine store you have here, Mr. Potter.

POTTER

That's me. We sell about everything here.

At the phone booth, MEINIKE rifles panickily through the phone book. WILSON takes a look at him and leaves. MEINIKE finds a number and memorizes it.

POTTER is still chuckling at the radio broadcast. MEINIKE comes up to the counter and puts his bag down on it.

MEINIKE

This suitcase—I could leave it here?

POTTER

I don't assume no responsibility. Just put it up on that shelf. It'll be there when you want it.

MEINIKE puts his bag on the shelf and leaves. WILSON reappears in the window, with a magazine.

WILSON

I'll buy this magazine. What's the best hotel in town?

POTTER

The best place to stay is Mrs. Peabody's. It's just down the road here a piece.

On the street, WILSON sees MEINIKE and follows after him—in the opposite direction to the one that POTTER has indicated.

POTTER

This way, Mister.

WILSON

Yes, thank you.

But WILSON continues to follow MEINIKE. MEINIKE knows that he is being followed and quickens his pace. He dashes across the street and is almost hit by an oncoming car. The car halts and honks. MEINIKE goes on, followed by WILSON.

On another street, MEINIKE looks around in panic for a place to run to. We see a concrete post with the sign "Harper School for Boys." MEINIKE goes up the stairs to an unlocked door at the top, opens it, and goes in, closing the door behind him.

WILSON, below, has missed MEINIKE but looks up at the door and goes up the stairs too. He closes the door behind him.

Inside the school, MEINIKE goes into a gym, followed by WILSON. MEINIKE stops in front of a couple of fire extinguishers; an axe is hung in the middle. MEINIKE goes to take down the axe but thinks better of it and moves on.

WILSON enters the gymnasium. Above, on a mezzanine, we see MEINIKE. Two gymnastics rings are hanging on chains near him. MEINIKE swings one down and hits WILSON on the head. WILSON falls down unconscious. MEINIKE flees through a mezzanine door.

The scene changes to a street with a house in front of it. MARY is standing in the window, hanging curtains. MEINIKE goes up to the house and knocks. MARY opens. MEINIKE barges in and closes the door while saying:

                    MEINIKE

Can I come in?

                     MARY

Yes, of course!

MEINIKE peers apprehensively through the curtain on the
door. He goes into the hallway.

                    MEINIKE

Does Mr. Charles Rankin live here?

                     MARY

Yes, he does, but he isn't here right now.

                    MEINIKE

Are you expecting him?

                     MARY

Yes, in a few minutes.

                    MEINIKE

How soon?

                     MARY

A few minutes.

                    MEINIKE

How soon?

                     MARY

A few minutes.

MEINIKE takes off his hat.

MEINIKE

I may wait here?

MARY

Yes, if you like. Would you like to sit down?

MEINIKE

Thank you.

MEINIKE sits down in a chair in the corner. MARY picks up the curtains she was hanging.

MARY

Are you a friend of Mr. Rankin?

MEINIKE

Yes, a friend.

MARY

I'm Mary Longstreet. How do you do?

MEINIKE

How do you do?

MARY sets down the curtains on the ladder she was standing on.

MARY

Mr. Rankin ought to be here now. Sometimes he stays after class, but he'll be coming straight home today, I'm sure. This is our wedding day.

MEINIKE

You are getting married?

MARY

Yes, at six o'clock. I know it's most unconventional, my being here today, but I want to get these curtains up.

MEINIKE gets up uneasily and puts on his hat.

MEINIKE

When he comes, which way does he come?

MARY

From Webster Hall. It's the big building right over there, see?

MARY opens the curtains to show him.

MEINIKE

Thank you.

He goes out.

MARY

But who should I say—?

But MEINIKE has left before she can finish.

We now see RANKIN walking down a school sidewalk in front of the chapel. As he passes, MEINIKE accosts him from behind a bush.

MEINIKE

Franz! It's me, Franz!

RANKIN

Meinike! We mustn't be seen talking together. Go back into the church—into the woods! Follow the path; I'll meet you there.

MEINIKE obediently goes off. Four STUDENTS come up to RANKIN from behind.

STUDENT #1

Hello, Professor Rankin!

RANKIN

Hello, men. What are you up to?

STUDENT #1

Paper chase. I go ahead and lay the trail.

STUDENT #2

You oughta have Jerry's job, Professor Rankin. Take a little off that waistline.

STUDENT #3

You ought to go with us, Mr. Rankin.

RANKIN

Where to?

STUDENT #2

The woods.

An attractive BLONDE goes by in the background. The STUDENTS whistle.

RANKIN

The woods? I'd like to, but I'm afraid I have a couple of other things to attend to.

STUDENT #1

Join us later. We'll be out till dark.

RANKIN

All right.

STUDENT #1

We'll catch up with you.

In the woods, STUDENT #1 is throwing paper; the other STU-DENTS are following him.

Elsewhere in the woods, MEINIKE comes up to RANKIN, who embraces him.

RANKIN

Meinike!

MEINIKE

Yes, Meinike.

RANKIN

I thought—

MEINIKE

I had been hanged—the others, but not I.

RANKIN

You haven't much changed—put you back in your old uniform, you'd look very much the same.

MEINIKE

Franz, I'm a different man from before.

RANKIN

I too. I too am different. I've changed a lot, Conrad. You know I gathered and destroyed every single item in Germany and Poland that might provide a clue to my identity. Guess what I'll be doing at six o'clock tonight? Standing before a minister of the Gospel, with a woman standing by me—the daughter of a justice of the United States Supreme Court, a famous liberal. The girl is even good to look at. Yes, the camouflage is perfect. Who would think that I was the notorious Franz Kindler in the sacred precincts of the Harper School, surrounded by the scions of America's first families? I'll stay hidden until the day we strike again.

> **MEINIKE**
> Franz! There will be another war?

> **RANKIN**
> Of course.

> **MEINIKE**
> War is an abomination. That is why I am here. That is why they released me. They set me free so that I could come . . .

> **RANKIN**
> Who set you free?

> **MEINIKE**
> The Almighty.

> **RANKIN**
> You don't mean . . .

> **MEINIKE**
> I mean God!

RANKIN clutches him by the arm and laughs.

> **RANKIN**
> Come!

MEINIKE

Franz, I'm a new man since I—

RANKIN

You, Conrad, religious!

MEINIKE

Franz, all doors were open to me! All the doors! It was one of God's miracles!

RANKIN

Mm . . . hmm.

RANKIN pauses as he realizes the truth.

RANKIN

They freed you so you could lead them to me. Have you been followed? Were you followed here?

MEINIKE

Yes!

RANKIN

Who followed you?

MEINIKE

The evil one! He looked like any other man. He was dressed just like any other man. He even smoked a pipe! I recognized him. And I killed him. I hit him. God's will be done.

RANKIN

You killed him—the man with the pipe?

MEINIKE

Yes.

RANKIN

The man who followed you? No one else followed you?

They walk on.

RANKIN

Mm-hm. Mm-hm.

MEINIKE

You must be brought to salvation, Franz. Confess your sins, as I have. Proclaim your guilt! Only thus you can obtain salvation.

RANKIN

You really think so, Conrad?

MEINIKE

The strength can only come from God.

RANKIN

Mm-hmm.

MEINIKE

Kneel, my new friend, and together we will pray to him to give you strength.

But they do not kneel. MEINIKE removes his hat.

MEINIKE (PRAYING)

I have sinned against heaven, and before Thee. I am not worthy to be called Thy son. Say these words after me: I despair of my sins.

RANKIN

I despair of my sins.

MEINIKE

O God of all holiness, how could I have ever offended thee?

RANKIN takes MEINIKE by the neck.

RANKIN

. . . of all goodness . . .

RANKIN strangles MEINIKE.

STUDENT'S VOICE

This way, fellas! And don't let him get away!

RANKIN runs off.

The STUDENT runs past the bush where MEINIKE's body lies and goes on.

RANKIN drags MEINIKE's body off the path and covers it hastily with dirt. He runs off in panic to the site where he and MEINIKE stood talking and cover the tracks with dirt as well. He picks up some of the paper chase papers and strews them in another direction.

STUDENT'S VOICE

Hey, fellas!

Two other STUDENTS run after the first one, past MEINIKE's body, which they do not notice. RANKIN runs off.

STUDENT

This way, fellas!

The scene shifts to a church, where RANKIN and MARY are standing before a CLERGYMAN. JUDGE LONGFELLOW is at MARY's right; LAWRENCE is at RANKIN's left.

CLERGYMAN

Dearly beloved, we are gathered in the sight of God and in the face of this company to join together this man and this woman in holy matrimony.

The scene now shifts back to the gym, where WILSON is lying, recovering consciousness. His pipe is lying before him. He picks it up distractedly and stumbles to his feet.

Back in the church:

CLERGYMAN

. . . And forsaking all others, be faithful to her alone, as long as ye both shall live?

RANKIN

I will.

CLERGYMAN

Mary, wilt thou have this man for thy husband to live together after God's ordinance in the holy estate of matrimony? Wilt thou love him, honor him, comfort him, keep him, in sickness and in health, forsaking all others, keeping only unto him, so long as ye both shall live?

MARY

I will.

In the main square of Harper, WILSON walks along, touching his head, which is still in pain. He goes into the drugstore. POTTER is at the counter.

WILSON

Afternoon.

POTTER

Afternoon.

Through the window, across the green, WILSON sees the wedding party.

WILSON

Wedding?

POTTER

Yeah. Judge Longstreet's daughter. He's a Supreme Court justice, you know.

WILSON goes to the counter.

WILSON

Bottle of aspirin, please.

POTTER
(pointing)

Right back there, third shelf down from the top. You'll see the big one's on the left, the economy size. You've got to get it yourself, Mister. Right back there.

WILSON goes toward the aspirin.

POTTER

All your needs are on our shelves. Just look around and help yourself. Right, down that shelf. That's it.

WILSON reaches onto a shelf and removes a bottle.

POTTER

Living down at Mrs. Peabody's?

• **22** •

WILSON

Just for a few days only.

WILSON approaches the counter.

WILSON

Coffee too, please. Or should I get it myself?

CUSTOMER AT COUNTER

Cafeteria style around here.

POTTER

That's right: self-service. Three dollars even.

WILSON

What about the cream?

POTTER

Folks around here take it black.

.

WILSON goes to a coffee urn.

CUSTOMER

The one on the right.

WILSON pours himself a cup.

WILSON

Thank you.

> (now behind counter,
> drawing a cup of coffee)

Who's Miss Longstreet marrying?

MR. POTTER

One of the teachers down at the school.

FEMALE CUSTOMER

Stranger in town.

POTTER

I issued the license.

WILSON

*(interestedly, coming around
opposite Potter, carrying cup)*

Oh?

MR. POTTER

Yeah. I'm town clerk.

WILSON comes up to the counter, where there is a checker-board.

POTTER

Checkers?

WILSON

All right.

WILSON sits down in front of the counter to play.

WILSON

Town clerk, huh? Well, must be quite a responsibility!

POTTER
(*making move*)

Town clerk runs the town, you might say . . . We usu-
ally make it for 15, 20—we often play as high as 25¢
a game.

WILSON

Kind of stiff for me, but I'll take a fire. Make a million,
lose a million.

POTTER

That's the way it goes. My move.

WILSON

All right . . . You must know just about everybody in
town here?

POTTER

Not just about. Know everybody.

(*his tone changing*)

Are you here on business?

(*Wilson nods*)

WILSON

Uh-huh.

POTTER

School business?

WILSON shakes his aching head.

POTTER

Sellin' somethin'?

Again WILSON shakes his head.

Buyin'?

WILSON's eyes search the room. They see a sign. It announces
a sale of antiques. WILSON points to it.

MR. POTTER

Oh . . . antique dealer. They all come to Harper.

(Wilson nods)

Judge Longstreet's got the best collection in these
parts. Won't do you no good, though.

WILSON

No. I don't suppose he'd sell.

(casually)

Happen to know if there are any other out-of-town
buyers here?

MR. POTTER

Come to think of it, there was a fella come in this
morning. He came on the same bus with you. Left his
suitcase here, never did come back for it. He might
be one of them. But no . . . no, he was more of a mis-
sionary type. Wasn't in here but a minute. Just looked
in the phone book. Tiny little fella, he was. Thinnish.
Unfortunate-looking.

WILSON takes off his hat and rubs his head painfully.

POTTER

Hurt your head, Mister?

WILSON

No, nothing serious.

WILSON makes a bad move on the checkerboard.

POTTER

That's too bad.

POTTER triumphantly jumps five men. WILSON looks startled.

MR. POTTER

(with great unction and satisfaction)

In this game, you gotta keep your mind going. 25 cents, please.

DISSOLVE TO:
INT. LONGSTREET HOME—NIGHT

The wedding reception is in progress. Most of Harper is present, both school and town.

CAMERA, on CRANE, MOVES THROUGH THE CROWD WITH MARY, who still carries her bridal bouquet. She stops by old MRS. LAWRENCE.

MRS. LAWRENCE

I won't pretend I'm not disappointed . . .

Mary comes to a group surrounding JUDGE LONGSTREET, which includes NOAH.

MARY

Has anyone seen my brand-new husband?

JUDGE LONGSTREET

Don't tell me he's deserted you already.

MARY
(pushing back his lock of hair)

Looks as if. The brute.

She turns to find her Irish setter, RED, at her heels.

Red . . . where's Charles? Go find Charles! Go on! Hurry up!

The dog runs off obediently.

DISSOLVE TO:
EXT. WOODS—NIGHT—CLOSE SHOT

RANKIN is finishing filling up a grave with MEINIKE's body. He covers it with leaves. Realizing that he still has MEINIKE's hat, he hastily covers it with some leaves and dirt.

DISSOLVE TO:
INT. LONGSTREET HOME—NIGHT

NOAH is reporting to MARY, who stands beside JUDGE LONG-STREET.

NOAH

I've looked everywhere for him, Mary And I can't find him.

MARY

But where could he be? I'm getting worried.

RANKIN'S VOICE
(over scene)

Are you, darling? What about?

CAMERA PULLS BACK to include RANKIN as he reaches her side. He wears a slack suit.

MARY

Oh . . . you've changed.

RANKIN

Don't you think you'd better? Weren't we supposed to go on a honeymoon or something?

MARY

Just give me five minutes.

MARY rushes out of the room.

INSERT—A PAGE

It is headed "Arrivals in Harper last 12 months." Beneath this are six names, through the top four of which a thin line has been drawn. The fifth and sixth names on the page are SAUNDERS SCUDDER and CHARLES RANKIN. Entries after the names establish their occupations as teachers at the Harper School.

INT. WILSON'S ROOM—DAY

WILSON tilts back in his chair, frowning thoughtfully. His eyes wander out the window. What he sees jerks him upright.

THE VILLAGE SQUARE

WILSON is looking straight across at the clock tower. The hands of the clock move . . . stop . . . move again . . . and stop.

INT. WILSON'S ROOM

WILSON whirls from the window, shoves the papers on table into his pocket, snatches up his hat, and exits.

INT. CHURCH

WILSON, removing hat, enters, crosses the length of the church and starts up the stairs leading into the belfry . . . CAMERA following.

INT. BELFRY

WILSON ascends and goes up two flights. He sees NOAH above him.

INT. CLOCK TOWER

WILSON sees NOAH, back turned, wiping the clock's works with a cloth. WILSON comes forward as NOAH, surprised at the interruption, faces him.

WILSON

Hello there.

NOAH

(politely)

Hello.

WILSON

(examining the works)

Is that you working upon there on the clock?

NOAH

No, sir. I'm just cleaning around it.

WILSON

Beautiful clock, beautiful, from what I could see out front!

(casually)

Oh, by the way, my name's Wilson.

NOAH

I'm Longstreet, Noah Longstreet.

WILSON

(he and NOAH shake hands)

Glad to know you. I couldn't tell from out front, but I would say that it was late 16th century. Probably by Hobrecht of Strasbourg. You know, the clock.

NOAH

I wouldn't know. My brother-in-law is going to work on it.

WILSON

Oh. Is he up there now?

NOAH

No, he's on his honeymoon. He plans to work on it when he gets back.

WILSON

Oh. Is he an expert?

NOAH
(shrugging)

Yes, but it's really more of a hobby with him.

WILSON

Really? It is with me too. Honeymoon?

NOAH

Yes. He and my sister . . . He has to be back on Friday because of examinations. He's one of the teachers at the school. His name is Rankin.

WILSON

Oh?

DISSOLVE TO:
INT. LONGSTREET LIVING ROOM—
NIGHT

WILSON is examining a silver inkstand, with JUDGE LONG-STREET and NOAH standing next to him.

JUDGE LONGSTREET

It's nice to show it to somebody who knows what Revere silver's all about. But, personally, my specialty is pewter.

WILSON
*(a little absently-not wanting to get caught
on a subject he's not boned up on)*

Yes . . . pewter.

*(then, brightening, as he remembers a quote
from the book he's been studying)*

The Revere workmanship, although sometimes heavy
in design, almost invariably shows the sign of a mas-
ter craftsman. This is beautiful.

**MARY and RANKIN come in. MARY comes up to NOAH and
embraces him.**

MARY

Noah.

She kisses her father.

MARY

Adam.

JUDGE LONGSTREET

Mr. Wilson, my daughter Mary. My son-in-law, Charles
Rankin.

WILSON shakes MARY's and RANKIN's hands.

MARY

How do you do.

WILSON

How do you do. I hope you won't mind my intruding on
your homecoming.

SARA and LAWRENCE enter.

LAWRENCE

Good evening, Mary.

                            MARY

Jeff, how are you! You're looking good.

LAWRENCE and MARY hug.

                            SARA

Welcome home, Miss Mary. Dinner is served.

To SARA's embarrassed delight, MARY embraces her.

                            MARY

Hello, Sara.

                            SARA
                          (squirming)

If you don't set down, it'll get cold!

                    JUDGE LONGSTREET

Well, sister, how were the mountains?

                            MARY

They were perfectly marvelous!

                      TRAVELING SHOT

CAMERA MOVES AHEAD OF THEM as they move into the
DINING ROOM, where a table is set. MARY sits at one head of
the table, facing JUDGE LONGSTREET.

                            MARY

Mr. Wilson, will you come sit here on my right? Jeff, in
your usual place, and darling, you're right there.

They all sit down.

MARY

You ought to see Charles on skis. He's absolutely wonderful!

RANKIN

No . . .

MARY

Yes, darling, you are. And I'm pretty good too, aren't I?

RANKIN

Very.

MARY

Well, for a beginner.

LAWRENCE

Did you remember to keep your knees together and your apparatus in?

MARY

Yes, Jeff, I did.

JUDGE LONGSTREET

Mr. Wilson here is compiling a catalogue of Paul Revere silver.

NOAH
(to Rankin)

Mr. Wilson is also an authority on clocks.

RANKIN, sipping his soup, pauses momentarily.

MARY

Really! Why, that's Charles's hobby.

WILSON

Yes, so your brother tells me.

(turning to Rankin)

I understand you're going to fix the one in the church tower?

RANKIN

I may try.

WILSON

Quite an undertaking.

MARY

To show the kind of wife I am, I hope he fails. I like Harper just that way is . . . even to the clock that doesn't run.

As the scene progresses, SARA moves around the table, serving dinner. RED, the setter dog, has followed them into the room and settled himself beside MARY.

RANKIN

How long have you been in Harper, Mr. Wilson?

WILSON

Since Friday, a week ago.

LAWRENCE

(looking up quickly)

You've lost a day. I patched you up on Friday. By the way, how's the head?

WILSON

Very much improved, thanks to you, Doctor.

LAWRENCE

You were hurt on Thursday. The day of the wedding.

RANKIN's fork poises midway to its destination.

WILSON

Yes, that's right. Wednesday I left Bangor.

RANKIN

You were hurt, Mr. Wilson?

WILSON

Oh, nothing serious.

LAWRENCE

Serious enough to raise a bump on his head the size
of a billiard ball.

RANKIN's last doubts are removed. This is the Devil that pursued MEINIKE to Harper.

WILSON

(to the table at large)

The usual door.

RED raises up on his haunches and puts his head on MARY's
lap.

JUDGE LONGSTREET

Good thing you're back, Sister. That dog of yours has
been inconsolable.

MARY

(lifting a scrap of meat from her plate)

That's for missing me, Red.

(she turns to her father)

There's a good boy. How was your meeting, Adam?

JUDGE LONGSTREET

Irritating . . .

(explaining to WILSON)

The Foreign Policy Association.

NOAH

I read that fellow's report.

JUDGE LONGSTREET

Yes, Standish.

NOAH

I think he's full of prunes.

JUDGE LONGSTREET

That's the way we used to talk in the 1930s, Noah.

LAWRENCE

Standish?

WILSON

The *London Times* man in Berlin.

JUDGE LONGSTREET

Of course he was quoting rumors, mostly. Men drilling by night . . . underground meeting places . . . pagan rituals.

NOAH

Do you believe them, Pop?

JUDGE LONGSTREET

Anything's possible.

LAWRENCE

I'm sorry, sir, but I think it's ridiculous. There may be some fanatics, but no German in his right mind could still have any taste for war.

WILSON

Do you know Germany, Mr. Rankin?

RANKIN

(easily)

I'm sorry. I have a way of making enemies on that subject. It's pretty unpopular.

WILSON

We shall consider it the objective opinion of an objective historian.

RANKIN

A historian? A psychiatrist could explain it better. The German sees himself as the innocent victim of world envy and hatred . . . conspired against, set upon by inferior peoples, inferior nations.

*(Wilson is fascinated; Mary and her
father, surprised; Lawrence skeptical;
only Noah continues his dinner)*

RANKIN

He cannot admit to error, much less to wrongdoing. Not the German. We chose to ignore Ethiopia and Spain. But we learned from our casualty lists the price of looking the other way . . .

. . . Men of truth everywhere have come to know for whom the bell tolled. But not the German. He still follows his warrior gods, marching to Wagnerian strains, his eyes still fixed upon the fiery sword of Siegfried.

(he pauses, glances from one face
to the other, ending on Wilson)

In those subterranean meeting places . . . that you don't believe in . . . the German's dream world comes alive, and he takes his place in shining armor beneath the banners of the Teutonic Knights. Mankind is waiting for the Messiah. But for the German, the Messiah is not the Prince of Peace. He's another Barbarossa, another Hitler.

WILSON

Then you have no faith in the reforms that are being effected in Germany.

RANKIN

I don't know, Mr. Wilson. I can't believe that people can be reformed except from within. The basic principles of equality and freedom never have and never will take root in Germany.

(continuing eagerly)

The will to freedom has been voiced in every other tongue . . . "All men are created equal." "Liberté, égalité, fraternité . . ." In German . . .

NOAH

(interrupting quietly)

There's Marx: "Proletarians, unite. You have nothing to lose but your chains."

RANKIN

But Marx wasn't a German. Marx was a Jew.

JUDGE LONGSTREET

My dear Charles . . . if we concede your argument . . .
there is no solution.

RANKIN

Once again, I differ.

WILSON

What is it then?

RANKIN

Annihilation . . . down to the last babe in arms.

MARY

(disturbed . . . a little worried)

Charles . . . I can't imagine you're advocating a Car-
thaginian peace.

RANKIN

(smiling)

Well, as an historian, I must remind you the world
hasn't had much trouble with Carthage in the past
two thousand years.

WILSON looks extremely disturbed.

JUDGE LONGSTREET

There speaks our pedagogue . . .

MARY
(brightening)

Speaking of teachers, Mr. Wilson, the faculty is coming to tea next Tuesday. If you have nothing better to do, would you like to join us?

WILSON

I'd like to, but my work here is finished. I'm leaving Harper tomorrow.

DISSOLVE TO:
INT. RANKIN HOUSE—NIGHT

MARY and RANKIN enter. RANKIN closes the door and turns on the lights as MARY says:

MARY

Extraordinary, isn't it . . . clocks being Mr. Wilson's hobby too?

RANKIN

Yes, isn't it?

RED comes up to them.

MARY

Well, Red, how do you like your new home?

(Red wags his tail)

RANKIN

He loves it. Come on, Red, I'll take you for a walk.

MARY

You don't have to walk him. Just let him out. He won't
run off.

RANKIN

I'm restless. I need the walk. Come along, Red.

MARY turns and starts up the stairs. RANKIN snaps his fingers for RED and goes out the door.

INT. WILSON'S BEDROOM—NIGHT

He is sitting at the phone in his shirtsleeves.

WILSON
(into telephone)

I'll be in Washington tomorrow afternoon. You were
right about Rankin. He's above suspicion.

DISSOLVE:
EXT. THE RANKIN HOUSE—NIGHT

RANKIN comes out, closing the door behind him. Then, with
long, hurried strides, he moves unhesitatingly towards the
woods. RED follows him.

DISSOLVE TO:
EXT. THE WOODS—NIGHT

Rankin enters and, as he finds MEINIKE's grave undisturbed,
his face lights up with relief. Then, CAMERA MOVING AHEAD
OF HIM, he turns and starts for home. After a few paces, he
realizes that RED is not at his heels. He turns and snaps his
fingers. When RED fails to appear, he whistles. Then:

RANKIN

Here, Red . . . Red, come here . . .

He waits a moment. RED does not appear. He starts back whence he came.

Beside MEINIKE's grave, RANKIN reenters and looks towards the grave. His eyes narrow.

RANKIN sees RED, his forepaws industriously digging into the earth, the leaves scattered in all directions. RED continues his digging as RANKIN watches him. RANKIN tries to chase him off, but RED keeps going back to the grave. RANKIN kicks out with all his strength, hitting RED in the ribs, and falling down himself. At the moment of contact:

INT. WILSON'S ROOM—NIGHT

WILSON, lying in bed, suddenly sits bolt upright as though awakened by RANKIN's kick.

He switches on a light and gets to his feet. Then hurries to the desk, seats himself, and picks up the phone.

WILSON
(into phone)

Uh . . . Get me long distance . . . I want Washington, D. C. . . .

EXT. WOODS—NIGHT

RANKIN is having a cigarette to calm himself.

INT. WILSON'S ROOM—NIGHT

WILSON is continuing his telephone conversation.

WILSON
(into phone)

. . . Well . . . who but a Nazi would deny that Karl Marx was a German because he was a Jew . . . I think I'll stick around for a while.

*(hangs up receiver and sits staring
out the window thoughtfully)*

DISSOLVE TO:
INT. RANKIN BEDROOM—NIGHT

RANKIN, in pajamas and dressing gown, emerges from the dressing room, casting a long shadow on the sleeping MARY. He stands for a second, looking down at the sleeping figure of his wife. The lights, from the room beside him shine across her bed. In her sleep, she stirs fitfully and whimpers, child-like. Suddenly her body jerks spasmodically and she is awake. She stares up at her husband, frightened.

RANKIN

What is it, dear?

MARY
(dazedly)

I'm sorry, I was dreaming.

(brushing her hand across her eyes)

About that little man.

                          RANKIN
                      (sitting beside her)

What little man?

                           MARY

I told you about him . . . he came here . . . the day we
were married.

                    (she shakes her head)

Light me a cigarette, honey.

                          RANKIN
                     (lighting one for her)

Oh . . . yes. I remember.

He hands her the lighted cigarette. She puffs on it gratefully.

                           MARY

I never had a dream like that before. It frightened me.
The little man was walking, all by himself, across a
deserted city square. Wherever he moved, he threw
a shadow. But when he moved, Charles, the shadow
stayed behind him, and spread out just like a carpet.

                  *(she stops, takes another puff
                   on the cigarette . . . then, with
                     an abrupt change of tone)*

I wish you could think who he might have been.

                          RANKIN

You're overtired.

                           MARY

Perhaps.

(smiling at him, handing him her cigarette.)

Here, put this out, will you?

There is the whimpering bark of a dog. She starts in surprise.

MARY

What was that?

RANKIN doesn't answer. The howl is heard again.

MARY

Why, that sounded like Red, Charles.

(she starts getting out of bed)

What in the world is the matter with him?

RANKIN
(quietly)

I have put him in the cellar.

MARY
(startled)

No wonder he's howling. He's never been locked up in his entire life.

RANKIN

But if he's to live with us, he must be trained. At night, he will sleep in the cellar. In the daytime, he will be kept on a leash.

RED howls again, the sound dying away in a moan.

MARY
(facing him)

Charles, I don't believe in dogs being treated like prisoners. And he's *my* dog.

RANKIN
(gently)

Please, Mary . . . I know what's best . . .

Their eyes stay met for a long moment. Finally, a decision reached, MARY lies down. RANKIN kisses her and leaves. MARY lies awake, looking worried.

FADE OUT:

FADE IN:
EXT.

NOAH is sitting in a boat in front of a tackle shop. WILSON comes up to him, RED running in front of him.

WILSON

Hi there, Red! I thought you'd gone to live with your mistress!

NOAH

Mary brought him home. Said he howls all night.

WILSON

Ah. Fishing any good in these parts?

NOAH

Pretty fair. Like to come along?

WILSON

Well, I'm afraid I've got the wrong clothes on, but the
fish probably won't mind. Thank you.

**WILSON and NOAH are in the boat. NOAH has his fishing line
out. Then he reels it in and puts the rod away in the boat.**

NOAH

I'm just not lucky today, that's all.

NOAH holds out a candy bar.

NOAH

Would you like a candy bar?

WILSON

I don't mind if I do. Thank you.

WILSON

All your folks like fishing?

NOAH

Oh, my dad's great. He always brings in something.

WILSON

What about Charles?

NOAH

(hesitates for a moment)

Charles? Oh! I have to call him Mr. Rankin in school.
I get a little mixed up sometimes. He spends most of
his time on the clock.

WILSON

Why don't you like him, Noah?

NOAH

What do you mean?

WILSON

You don't like your brother-in-law. It's none of my business, but I wish you'd tell me why.

NOAH

I like him well enough. No reason why I shouldn't.

WILSON

Don't tell me I'm butting in, because I know I am, but I
can't help myself. It's my business. I hate bringing you
into this, Noah, but you're the only one I can turn to.
I need your help very badly.

NOAH

What is it?

WILSON

Your sister may be in great trouble. I know that you're
man enough for what I'm going to ask you to do for
her. The truth is, I'm not really an antique dealer. I'm
sort of a detective.

WILSON and NOAH are getting out of the boat.

NOAH

What do you want me to do, Mr. Wilson?

WILSON

It would help me a lot if I knew every move Charles
Rankin made on the day of his wedding. Right up to
the ceremony itself.

NOAH
(frowning)

I should be able . . .

(a new thought)

. . . unless Charles realizes what I'm doing.

WILSON

I'll keep him busy.

They walk along the dock.

NOAH
(incredulity reasserting itself)

Gee, Mr. Wilson, you must be wrong. Mary wouldn't fall in love with that kind of a man.

WILSON

I hope I am wrong, Noah. But that's the way it is. People can't help who they fall in love with.

WILSON walks off. NOAH follows him uneasily with his eyes.

INT. POTTER'S—NIGHT

WILSON enters POTTER's drugstore.

Four HARPER BOYS enjoy their sodas at a table in the rear. WILSON goes around behind counter and fixes himself some coffee. POTTER sets up the checkers.

WILSON

Evening, Mr. Potter.

POTTER

Evening, Mr. Wilson.

One of the HARPER BOYS goes to POTTER to pay.

POTTER

Eighty-five cents.

WILSON sits down across from POTTER for a game of checkers.

POTTER

Hear you and Perfessor Rankin aim to fix the clock.

WILSON

That's right.

POTTER

Figure it'll tell time rightly?

(another nod)

And will the angel circle round the belfry?

(another nod)

Is that a man or a woman angel, Mr. Wilson?

WILSON

I don't know.

MR. POTTER

Well . . . reckon it don't make much difference 'mongst angels.

WILSON makes a move, enabling POTTER to take several of his men on the board.

POTTER

Give up?

WILSON

No, no, we'll play it out. That's my privilege: 25 cents. By the way, has Mr. Rankin picked up his supper this evening?

MR. POTTER

No. He kind of gets through up there about now.

WILSON

Yes . . . I know.

POTTER

Gets dark earlier these days.

WILSON looks at the shelf behind POTTER and sees MEINIKE's suitcase.

WILSON

Our little man never did pick up his suitcase, did he?

MR. POTTER

Nope.

WILSON

Strange.

MR. POTTER

Ain't it, though?

(he pauses, then:)

I've been tempted once or twice to look and see what's inside of it.

(he looks hopefully at Wilson)

It isn't even locked.

WILSON

Seems to me that, under the circumstances, you have
a perfect right.

MR. POTTER

You do? I wouldn't want to do it without a witness.

WILSON

That's me.

MR. POTTER

It is?

WILSON nods. POTTER reaches down, takes out the bag, and
places it on the counter. He rubs his palms together. He opens
the lid. As he does so, WILSON strikes a match and puts it to
his pipe. He does not look at the suitcase as POTTER fishes
through it.

POTTER

Wonder what's in it?

WILSON

Soiled linen . . . a sweater . . . soap and a razor wrapped
in a towel with "S. S. Cristobal" written across it . . . a
pair of old shoes . . . Nothing but religious pamphlets.

POTTER is too intent on what he is doing to note that WILSON
is not looking into the suitcase.

MR. POTTER

Yep . . . that's all.

THE DOOR OPENS, and MARY and RANKIN enter.

MARY

Good evening, Mr. Wilson . . . Mr. Potter.

WILSON

Good evening. Mr. Potter and I have been poking our noses into somebody else's business. That suitcase. That little chap left it here and never did call back.

MR. POTTER

That was more than two weeks ago.

RANKIN now knows this is MEINIKE's suitcase. He moves over to stand on the opposite side of MARY from WILSON.

MARY

(with normal interest)

Did he say what he was doing there?

MR. POTTER

Nope. Looked in the phone book but didn't telephone. Kind of scrawny-looking, with starey big blue eyes. Weird walk . . . like any second he might break into a run.

MARY

(with sudden excitement)

Did he have a foreign accent?

Beneath the counter, RANKIN's hand closes like a vise on her wrist. She turns to face him as POTTER replies. Their eyes meet, warning in RANKIN's. Wilson observes this.

MR. POTTER

Why, yes, he did. Not so much of an accent . . . as a foreign way of talking.

RANKIN's eyes, fixed on MARY's, glare briefly. Then, conscious of WILSON's interest, RANKIN looks down at the counter. But his hand on her wrist increases its pressure.

WILSON

Do you happen to know who he could be, Mrs. Rankin?

MARY

(forces a laugh)

Why, no . . . I was just trying to complete your mystery. Don't all foreign . . . strangers have foreign accents?

RANKIN looses his grip. They all turn towards the door as NOAH comes in.

NOAH

Mary, have you seen Red?

MARY

Why, no. Not since I took him home to you a couple of days ago.

NOAH

He's spending all his time out in the woods. Doesn't even come home for meals.

RANKIN

I thought you told me he never ran away.

NOAH

(answering for Mary)

He never did.

MARY

That's why Noah's so anxious.

(slips down from her stool)

Good night, Mr. Wilson, good night, Noah.

MARY leads the way out, RANKIN at her heels.

EXT. POTTER'S—NIGHT

WILSON and NOAH come out and see RANKIN and MARY go into the church.

NOAH

Were you able to find out anything?

WILSON

(nodding)

Meinike did go to Rankin's house. And your sister did see him.

They move down the street.

NOAH

Did Mary say so?

WILSON

She started to. Your sister is a fine woman, Noah. But she must find out what kind of man she's married to.

NOAH

You don't know Mary. She wouldn't listen to anything against him . . . much less believe.

WILSON

Noah, we must arrange it so that she finds out for herself. Do you understand?

NOAH nods.

One thing's certain, she knows nothing now . . . nothing at all . . . except that he didn't want her to admit having seen someone she did see. I'd give something to know what explanation he's making right now.

DISSOLVE TO:
INT. CHURCH—NIGHT

RANKIN and MARY are sitting in a pew.

RANKIN

I was a student at Geneva. There was a girl . . . The night before I was to leave, we went out on the lake together. She told me that unless I promised to marry her, she'd never return to shore. I thought she was joking, naturally. But she wasn't. Before I could stop her, she stood up in the boat and—well—I dived in after her, but it was too late: she was gone.

RANKIN

(he pauses)

Only one person knew we were out on that lake together. Her brother. He knew I hadn't murdered her, but he told me he was willing to call it an accident, for—compensation. I gave him what I had. As the years went by, I allowed myself to believe that the dead past really was dead.

(again he pauses)

Then, on our wedding day, Mary, he appeared again. Her brother was the little man. I gave him all the money I had in the world . . . and he went away again.

MARY

You should have told me . . . not carried this awful thing around by yourself.

RANKIN

You're a very wonderful person, Mary.

(He kisses her tenderly.)

And I love you very much.

MARY

Charles . . .

(he looks at her inquiringly)

. . . Why—why didn't he go back for his things?

RANKIN

(after a pause)

Well, I suppose, once he had money, he could afford better. Darling, I'm extremely nervous . . . I think I'll work alone on the clock. By myself. It will calm me . . . You understand, don't you?

MARY

(rising)

Of course I understand.

RANKIN

Shall I walk you home?

MARY

No, dear, there's no need of that.

                    RANKIN
                    (tenderly)

It's really late . . .

                     MARY

That's all right . . . In Harper, there's nothing to be
afraid of.

He kisses her again.

                    RANKIN

I love you.

She goes off. RANKIN looks after her apprehensively.

                EXT. OUTSIDE
           DR. LIVINGSTON'S HOUSE

The next day, NOAH is holding the dead body of RED. WILSON
is there, smoking his pipe.

                     NOAH

Poor old Red . . . He heard my whistle, I'll bet, but he
couldn't bark or anything. He just crawled this far
and died.

              (*His lips tremble threateningly.*
           To cover his emotion, he bends over,
          and pats the dead dog's head very gently)

. . . Why do you think he died?

                    WILSON

Let's go and find out.

WILSON and NOAH, still carrying RED, go into LAWRENCE's office, which is next to POTTER's drugstore.

RANKIN goes into POTTER's drugstore. POTTER is sitting at the counter. He is looking out the window and sees NOAH and WILSON. RANKIN opens a bottle of Coke and pours it into a glass.

POTTER

That's young Longstreet's dog. Looks like he's dead to me. They're taking him up to Dr. Lawrence's office. Do you know anything about it?

RANKIN makes an indistinguishable noise and guzzles the rest of his Coke.

POTTER

Checkers?

RANKIN

No.

RANKIN makes to leave.

POTTER

Hey! Coke's a nickel!

RANKIN goes back to the counter and pays him.

POTTER

Thank you, Mr. Rankin.

Outside, CAMERA, on CRANE, moves in on an office window. The lettering on it says, "Jeffrey Lawrence. Office hours . . ."

Through the window, we see WILSON, NOAH, and LAWRENCE looking at RED's body. LAWRENCE is holding a test tube. WILSON is holding a crumb of dried mud.

WILSON

Oh, doctor? How long could the dog have lived with that amount of poison in him?

LAWRENCE

Not more than a minute or so.

WILSON

Well, then, Red must have been poisoned within a few hundred yards of where you found him, Noah. And the latter part of the distance he must have been moving slower and slower.

(abruptly)

Thank you very much, Doctor.

NOAH

Yes . . . Thanks, Jeff.

They leave. LAWRENCE pulls a sheet over the dead dog.

EXT. POTTER'S—AFTERNOON

POTTER is leaning out over the counter of his newstand, directing his assistant, PEABODY, at work.

MR. POTTER

Mr. Peabody, would you please get that magazine rack
in and hurry up about it!

PEABODY

Yes, Mr. Potter.

POTTER sees WILSON and NOAH come out of LAWRENCE's
office next door.

POTTER

Afternoon, Mr. Wilson. Afternoon, Noah.

EXT. SQUARE—NOAH AND WILSON

NOAH
(absently)

Evenin', Mr. Potter.

CAMERA, on CRANE, precedes NOAH and WILSON as they
move across the square, walking toward the Harper Inn.

NOAH

What does the law say about this kind of murder? Is it
the same as killing a man? It ought to be. It's just as bad.

WILSON
*(showing Noah the piece
of dried mud in his hand)*

Forepaws muddy . . . No mud on hind.

(he crumbles it and looks at it)

Dry leaves mixed with the mud. Red must have been
digging somewhere in the woods.

NOAH

Have you got any idea what for, Mr. Wilson?

WILSON
(nodding)

A body, I think . . . Meineke's.

NOAH
(in horror)

The little man . . .

(Wilson nods)

Then . . .

(the thought is too monstrous for words)

INT. POTTER'S—EVENING

The shop is dark. POTTER is unlocking the door, letting in RANKIN, who rushes in distractedly. POTTER turns on the lights in the shop.

POTTER

You just caught me.

RANKIN

Anything wrong?

POTTER

Wrong? Oh, you mean, closin' up like this?

(Rankin nods)

Just goin' on the search. What were you after?

RANKIN

A can of machine oil . . . What search?

MR. POTTER

For the body.

(Rankin stiffens)

State police've deputized half the town . . . Just reach up there—Fourth shelf . . .

RANKIN

*(forcing himself to be casual
as he crosses to shelf)*

One misses the news . . . up in the clock tower. What body are they searching for?

POTTER

My bet is it's the feller that left his bag here. Scrawny little duck. Unhappy looking. I knew he'd come to a bad end. That oil'll be 15 cents, mister . . . or I'll just put it on your account.

RANKIN hurries out.

DISSOLVE TO:
RANKIN BEDROOM—NIGHT

On the bed, RANKIN is packing an open suitcase. MARY comes into the room.

MARY

(entering)

Sara told me you were up here . . .

(she breaks off, seeing him packing)

Why are you packing? Are we going somewhere?

RANKIN

We aren't, my dearest . . . I am.

MARY

What are you talking about?

RANKIN

As a rule, men leave their wives because they don't love them, but I . . . I must leave you because I do. Oh, you won't object once you know the kind of man you married.

MARY

But you *are* the man I married, and that's all that matters. I meant what I said . . . for better . . . for worse.

RANKIN
(harshly)

Even to killing Red?

MARY recoils instantly. RANKIN watches narrowly for her reaction.

MARY
(aghast)

You couldn't.

RANKIN doesn't answer.

MARY

It was an accident.

RANKIN

No, I meant to kill him. Murder can be a chain, Mary.
One link leading to another until it circles your neck.
Red was digging at the grave of the man I killed.
Yes . . . your little man . . .

MARY

(in a whisper)

You killed him?

RANKIN

With these hands.

(he holds them out to her)

The same hands that have held you close to me.

(again harshly)

Now are you satisfied to let me go?

MARY

(in an agonized voice)

Why? Why did you do it?

RANKIN

I'd have given him all I had . . . but his dreams were far
grander. He knew that your father was well-to-do . . .
He knew that Justice Longstreet would be glad to protect his daughter from any scandal by paying a few
thousand dollars.

(turns back to face her)

Oh, Mary, I should have gone away and lost myself in
a world where he could never find me. But . . .

(He looks at her for a long moment)

I loved you, and I was weak.

MARY

(she comes to his side, then softly)

Darling . . . if one of us goes, we both go. You would have shared half my trouble, if I'd had any. Charles, what is there to connect you with that man?

RANKIN

Nothing, actually. You're the only one that knows I knew him.

MARY

Then you have no need of fear . . . if I'm the only one who can speak.

RANKIN

But Mary, in failing to speak, you've become a part of the crime.

MARY

But I'm already a part of it, because I'm a part of you.

For the first time, RANKIN feels completely secure. He starts to sweep her into his arms. She yields herself willingly to him. Then some instinctive reaction that she herself doesn't understand makes her body tremble. RANKIN instantly pulls back . . . only his hands remaining on her arms.

RANKIN

And yet you shudder at the first touch of my hands, as though it is the touch of death.

MARY

(shaking her head)

It's nerves.

(forcing herself)

Hold me close, Charles. Hold me close.

She raises her lips to him. Watching her intently, he kisses her.

EXT. THE WOODS—NIGHT

Several cars have been driven in near the grave, their powerful headlights stabbing across the scene. A row of lanterns lines the area around MEINIKE's grave, which has been opened. A rope has been strung on stakes around it to keep the crowd from trampling around it. The exhumed body lies, under canvas, beside the grave. Uniformed state patrolmen are getting pictures of the scene.

POTTER is standing there in a checked flannel shirt.

POTTER

Mr. Peabody, go back to the town with the sheriff and open the coroner's office.

PEABODY

Yes, sir.

POTTER

I knew durn well it was the same feller. Of course, he's changed some—being buried in the earth does it. Evenin', Mr. Wilson. Evenin', Noah. A mess, ain't it?

WILSON and NOAH are on a little knoll, looking down at the scene. NOAH turns to WILSON.

NOAH

What'll we do about Mary? We can't leave her alone with him . . . now that we know.

WILSON

(smokes his pipe in silence, then:)

She realizes now that whatever story he told her about Meinike was false.

(he pauses)

Noah, I think your sister should be ready to hear the truth.

INT. RANKIN LIVING ROOM—NIGHT

MARY and RANKIN are sitting at a table; she is holding a cup of coffee.

MARY

Charles . . . will they make me look at the body?

RANKIN

I shouldn't think so.

MARY

Because I couldn't do it. I mean, I don't think I could. You seen, I've never seen a dead person. I . . .

She breaks off as SARA enters, vegetable dish in hand.

RANKIN

How many are you having to tea, Mary?

MARY

Twenty-eight, all together.

SARA

(glancing at Mary's coffee)

You didn't eat nothin' at dinner. You'll be fainting again, Miss Mary.

RANKIN

(to Mary)

Isn't that rather a lot? Twenty-eight for just you two?

SARA

No, we'll manage all right.

She exits into the kitchen.

MARY

I suppose I should . . .

RANKIN

Should what?

MARY

(numbly)

I don't know. I only know that I'm terrified of seeing anybody . . . of being seen.

RANKIN

(voice level)

Mary, you must get tight hold of yourself. If you're determine to go through with this thing, you must know what you are going to say at all times. Perfect naturalness at all times. Darling, really, listen to me. Darling, I am prepared to go to the police.

SARA comes in.

SARA

It's your father, Miss Mary. He wants to talk to you.

MARY

Yes, thank you, Sara.

MARY slips from her chair and goes to the telephone in the
hall just outside dining room. At the telephone:

MARY
(into phone)

Hello.

(pause)

Yes, I think so . . .

(again a pause)

Just a minute, and I'll see.

She holds her hand over the mouthpiece of the phone.

MARY

He wants me to come over.

RANKIN
(levelly)

Did he ask me too?

MARY
(shaking her head)

He said he wanted to see me alone.

RANKIN

There's nothing unusual about a father wanting to see
his daughter, is there? *Is there?*

MARY

No!

(into the phone)

All right, Adam. I'll be right over.

She hangs up and looks at her husband.

(to RANKIN)

Don't you think that's rather strange?

RANKIN

Strange? No, not strange at all.

(reassuringly)

Tell you what I'll do I'll go to the church and work on the clock while you're with your father. When you're through, you can come by and pick me up later.

MARY

Charles . . . I'm so afraid. It was so pointed . . . his wanting to see me alone. And his voice sounded so different.

RANKIN

(his hand on her hair)

You know what you're going to say?

Looking up at him, she nods slowly.

DISSOLVE TO:
INT. JUDGE LONGSTREET'S
STUDY—NIGHT

MARY enters JUDGE LONGSTREET's study. WILSON is at the door and closes it behind her. The room is dark; a film is running. WILSON shuts off the projector and turns on the lights. JUDGE LONGSTREET has been standing at his desk but comes over to her.

JUDGE LONGSTREET

(gravely)

Come in, Mary.

(he closes the door behind her,
smiles at her reassuringly)

Sit down, my dear.

MARY

(looks from her father to Wilson
and back to her father again)

Is something wrong?

JUDGE LONGSTREET

Mary . . . Mr. Wilson is here on a very serious matter and we must try to help him in every way possible. He wants to ask a few questions of you.

MARY

What do you want to know, Mr. Wilson?

WILSON

You know about the body that was discovered yesterday, Mrs. Rankin?

(Mary nods)

Did you ever meet the deceased?

MARY

No, no, I never met him.

WILSON

Have you seen the body, Mrs. Rankin?

MARY

No . . .

WILSON

Then how can you be sure you never met him?

MARY

(hesitates)

Of course I can't be certain . . .

(masking fear with a show of anger)

Mr. Wilson, do you suspect me of something. If so, what?

WILSON

Of shielding a murderer.

(he pauses, then with apparent irrelevance)

WILSON

Perhaps this picture will refresh your memory, Mrs. Rankin . . .

CLOSEUP—PHOTO OF MEINIKE IN CIVILIAN CLOTHING.

WILSON

(Over Scene)

Do you recognize this man? That is Conrad Meinike. Commander in charge of one of the more efficient concentration camps. You know him, don't you? You *have* met him here in Harper . . .

MARY

No, no, I've never seen that man, Mr. Wilson.

JUDGE LONGSTREET has an extremely grave look on his face.

WILSON

Judge, would you mind turning out the lights?

JUDGE LONGSTREET goes to shut them off.

WILSON

I've been showing your father some films, Mrs. Rankin, and I'd like you to see them too. I'm on the Allied Commission for the Punishment of War Criminals. It's my job to bring escaped Nazis to justice. It's that job that brought me to Harper.

The screen shows a pile of exterminated bodies.

MARY

Surely you don't think . . . Mr. Wilson, I've never so much as even seen a Nazi.

WILSON

You might, without realizing it. They look like other people and act like other people—when it's to their benefit.

Mary doesn't answer.

We now see the film on the screen, of an empty gas chamber.

WILSON'S VOICE
(over scene)

. . . A gas chamber, Mrs. Rankin . . . the candidates were first given hot showers so that their pores would be open and the gas would act that much more quickly.

MARY looks up, the flickering of the screen reflected on her face, then back to screen.

We now see a shot of some GIs standing at the entrance to a lime pit. WILSON is silhouetted against the screen.

That is a lime pit in which hundreds of men, women, and children were buried alive.

MARY
*(unable to take her
eyes from the screen)*

Why do you wish me to look at these horrors?

WILSON
All this you've seen: it's all the product of one mind . . . the mind of a man named Franz Kindler.

MARY
(trying to identify the name)

Franz Kindler . . .

WILSON
Yes, he was one of the most brilliant of the younger minds of the Nazi party. It was Kindler who conceived the theory of genocide—mass depopulation of conquered countries, so that regardless of who won the war, Germany would emerge the strongest nation in Western Europe, biologically speaking.

He pauses. Her eyes go back to the screen.

WILSON

Unlike Goebbels and Himmler and the rest of them, Kindler had a passion for anonymity. The newspapers carried no picture of him. Oh, no. And, just before he disappeared, he destroyed every evidence that might link him with his past, down to the last fingerprint. There is no clue to the identity of Franz Kindler . . . except one little thing . . . He has a hobby that almost amounts to a mania . . . clocks.

MARY

So have lots of people . . . you . . . yourself.

WILSON

(ignoring her question)

Well, I'm not quite finished, Mrs. Rankin. In prison in Czechoslovakia, a war criminal was awaiting execution. This was Conrad Meinike, one-time executive officer of Franz Kindler. He was an obscenity on the face of the earth. The stench of burning flesh was in his clothes. But we gave him his freedom on the chance that he might lead me to Kindler. He led me here, Mrs. Rankin. And here, I lost him . . . until yesterday. Your dog, Red, found him for me. But unfortunately Meinike was dead and buried . . . Now, in all the world, there is only one person who can identify Franz Kindler. That person is the one who knows . . . knows definitely . . . who Meinike came to Harper to see.

The last frames of film run through the projector and the loose end flaps monotonously against the still turning reel. The bright light shines full on the screen. WILSON ignores it.

MARY
(finally . . . almost moaning)

No! . . . He's not a Nazi! My Charles is not a Nazi!

Now WILSON snaps on the room lights and turns off the projector.

MARY has risen and opened the door to the second-floor porch, WILSON and JUDGE LONGSTREET following.

INT. SECOND FLOOR PORCH—NIGHT

WILSON
(pounding at her)

You were at Rankin's house during the afternoon of the day you were married?

MARY

Where?

WILSON

Rankin's house.

MARY
(gasping)

Yes, yes.

WILSON

Did anyone come while you were there?

MARY

Not that I remember.

WILSON

Try to remember. It was not so long ago—only two weeks.
You were hanging curtains.

MARY

No one came.

WILSON

Were you alone all the time?

MARY

No.

WILSON

Who else was there?

MARY

Charles.

(with a great effort of will
she composes herself, then continues)

He came right after his last class, and we were together
for more than an hour. You have nothing to link my
husband with this man . . . Kindler . . . except a wild
suspicion. It's a ridiculous suspicion. You're trying to
use me to implicate him. You can't. You can't involve
me in a lie . . . That's all it is . . . a lie!

MARY dashes into the room from the porch and out the door.

JUDGE LONGSTREET

Mary, Mary! Wait a minute! Mary!

**We then see her running out of the front door of the house.
JUDGE LONGSTREET follows her.**

JUDGE LONGSTREET

Mary!

MARY keeps running.

JUDGE LONGSTREET

(calling to her from doorway)

Wait a minute, sister!

The use of the old term of affection stops her; she pauses, irresolute, then turns to face him. She runs into his arms, and he hugs her.

JUDGE LONGSTREET

That's better.

(he turns her to face him)

They walk along together. MARY is sobbing.

JUDGE LONGSTREET

You know that your welfare and Noah's means more to me than anything, don't you?

MARY

(her voice a little unsteady)

Yes, yes.

JUDGE LONGSTREET

We've got to face this thing with complete honesty, sister. Your entire happiness may well depend on your telling me the absolute truth.

(Mary begins to cry silently)

If Mr. Wilson is right and you have innocently married a criminal . . . then there is no marriage, and there is no call upon your loyalty as a wife.

MARY

He's good. He's good. Charles wouldn't hurt anybody . . . except to protect somebody he loves.

JUDGE LONGSTREET

In that case, the truth can't hurt him.

(she looks up at him.
His voice is very gentle.)

Charles was not with you that afternoon, sister. I remember your saying so when you came home.

MARY

(suddenly flying out)

You're against him too, Adam, yes you are! You've never liked him! That's why you won't believe me! Leave us alone, Adam! . . . He's my husband . . . He's not a Nazi! He's not one of those people . . . He's not! Leave us alone!

She runs away, her footsteps sounding on the graveled walk. JUDGE LONGSTREET looks after her sadly. Then the JUDGE hears WILSON's footsteps as he comes slowly down the graveled path. The JUDGE turns to face him. WILSON carries a case holding the projector.

WILSON

Well, she has the facts now, but she won't accept them. They're too horrible for her to acknowledge. Not so much that Rankin could be Kindler . . . as that she could ever have given her love to such a creature.

He starts walking, LONGSTREET moving too.

CAMERA precedes them to follow action.

WILSON

But we have one ally.

> (*Judge Longstreet looks at him,*
> *not understanding*)

Her subconscious. It knows what the truth is and is struggling to be heard. The will to truth within your daughter is much too strong to be denied.

JUDGE LONGSTREET
> (*thoughtfully*)

Look here, Wilson . . . if he's not Charles Rankin, we should be able to expose him without too much difficulty.

WILSON

I'm not interested in proving that he isn't Charles Rankin. I'm only interested in proving that he *is* Franz Kindler.

JUDGE LONGSTREET

How do you propose to do that?

As they walk, they come under a street light, their faces bright, then they pass by light and move off into darkness.

WILSON

Through your daughter.

> (*he hesitates*)

Unless I'm mistaken, she's headed for a breakdown. That's the usual result of a person being inwardly divided. Rankin will recognize this, and that's what I'm banking on.

JUDGE LONGSTREET

What do you mean?

WILSON

He can't afford to trust a person approaching hysteria. He won't. He'll have to act.

(dispassionately)

He may try to escape before she collapses. Which would be only an admission of guilt. Or . . .

JUDGE LONGSTREET

(impatiently)

Go on.

WILSON

(calmly)

He may kill her. You're shocked at my cold-bloodedness. That's quite natural. You're her father. It's because you are her father, Judge Longstreet, that I'm talking like this.

(he pauses)

Naturally, I shall try to prevent murder being done.

In the far background, the silhouette of the clock tower comes into view.

WILSON

However, the proof that murder is his aim would be the strongest evidence your daughter could have . . .

We now see the clock in the tower. It is telling the correct time—11:00—and two bronze figures—an angel and a devil—move mechanically around in front of it.

• **84** •

DISSOLVE TO:
INT. CLOCK TOWER—NIGHT

MARY is climbing up the ladder to the belfry. As she approaches the top, we see RANKIN above her, looking down. The clock is striking.

MARY

Charles!

RANKIN

Listen. It's striking! After a hundred years . . .

MARY

It was a trap . . . just like you said. Mr. Wilson was there. He tried to tell me that you were a Nazi . . . and I was supposed to believe it! Imagine . . . you . . . being an escaped Nazi. Oh, he thinks he's very clever, that Wilson. His idea was to horrify me into telling him about the little man.

RANKIN

Who did he say he thought I was?

MARY

A Nazi. Franz Kindler. He made it all up . . . just to trick me . . . but I didn't tell him anything. And I didn't tell Father anything. I outfaced them both of them, Charles. It'll be simple enough to prove you're not that . . . (she hesitates over the name) . . . that Nazi. We'll just find someone who was in your class at college. He'll identify you . . . and that's all there'll be to it.

RANKIN

If what you say is true, he can't touch me. I'm quite
safe . . . if you say nothing.

RANKIN is now hovering directly over MARY's head.

MARY

I won't, Charles . . . I promise I won't. They can torture
me, and I won't tell them anything.

OVERSCENE the sound of voices. Calls from the distance.
Below we see the citizens of Harper flocking to the church.

RANKIN

The chimes have awakened Harper. We must go
down and greet them. We must act naturally, smile at
them—you understand? Are you all right?

MARY

Yes, I'm all right. We'll face them, darling.

They start down the ladder.

DISSOLVE TO:
EXT. CHURCH—NIGHT

Six or eight townspeople have been called out by the chiming of the clock. Some are fully dressed, but most have hastily pulled on whatever was handiest. POTTER, overcoat over
pyjamas, occupies the forefront.

MR. POTTER

. . . and when she struck, that angel started marching. It was a sight to behold.

RANKIN and MARY emerge from the church. They are instantly surrounded.

FIRST MAN

Professor, you sure knocked it off. My hat's off to you.

SECOND MAN

Congratulations, Mr. Rankin.

WOMAN

Won't the Rector be delighted?

POTTER

What I want to know is, if it's going to chime all night long, how's a body going to get any sleep?

MARY

(to RANKIN)

We'll face them, darling . . . all of them.

POTTER

Them chickens is going to be off their roosts every fifteen minutes!

FADE OUT:

FADE INTO:
INT. RANKIN LIVING ROOM

It is now daytime. MARY rushes to draw the curtains.

MARY

Sara . . . I've told you, I want these curtains drawn. I don't like the sunlight streaming in.

(finishing closing them)

It's bad for them.

SARA

Miss Mary, that's rubbish and you know it. Up at the other house, we never drew a curtain in our lives.

MARY

That has nothing to do with it. This is my house, and I want them drawn.

SARA

(starting out)

Suit yourself. But it's certainly going to look mighty gloomy for the party.

MARY

(a momentary panic is in her eyes)

Is it that time already?

For answer, the doorbell rings.

SARA opens the door to admit two GUESTS, MRS. TINSDALL and MR. RANDALL, who enter.

MRS. TEASDALE

Did you see when they opened the grave, Mr. Randall? Was it too horrible?

MR. RANDALL

Well, not the most pleasant sight.

MRS. TEASDALE

There's Mary! Hello, Mary!

MARY smiles wanly and advances to greet her guests.

INT. POTTER'S—AFTERNOON

POTTER is handing RANKIN a bottle of prescription medicine.

MR. POTTER

Fillin' out prescriptions, that's one part of this business I hate; sleeping pills, that's another. $1.65. Want 'em wrapped?

RANKIN

No.

POTTER

Sleeping pills—don't approve of 'em. Man does a day's work, man gets a night's sleep.

Across the square, the clock strikes the quarter hour.

POTTER

Leastways, he could until that clock started bonging every few minutes.

RANKIN pockets the pills. He starts out. Then remembers something. Stops.

Oh . . . I believe Mrs. Rankin ordered some ice cream.

POTTER

Ice cream? Already gone.

RANKIN looks at him in surprise.

POTTER

A man said was he was goin' on to your house, so I gave it to him.

RANKIN

A man?

POTTER

Mr. Wilson!

RANKIN stiffens inwardly. Then, without a word, he hurries out of the store. POTTER looks after him in surprise.

*INT. RANKIN LIVING ROOM—
AFTERNOON*

The living room is crowded with GUESTS. WILSON is at the door, holding two bags of ice cream. SARA lets him in. WILSON hands her his hat.

WILSON

Mrs. Rankin.

Across the room, MARY sees WILSON and is startled as she stares at him. He walks across the room towards her.

MRS. TINSDALL

I'm absolutely terrified. I wouldn't dream of setting foot outside the house, unless Fred were along. Who knows . . . he might be anywhere . . . the murderer, I mean . . . waiting for a new victim.

WILSON comes forward easily to MARY. DR. HIBBARD is standing next to her.

WILSON

(taking her hand)

I hope you haven't forgotten you were kind enough to invite me, Mrs. Rankin.

MARY

(staring at him in disbelief)

No . . . No of course not, Mr. Wilson.

WILSON

(holding up the bags of ice cream)

Mr. Potter asked me to deliver this.

Before MARY can answer, NOAH appears beside them.

NOAH

Oh, the ice cream. Sara's waiting for it.

WILSON

I hope it hasn't melted.

NOAH takes the ice cream away.

WILSON

I won't detain you any longer.

LAWRENCE and DR. HIBBARD advance toward WILSON.

LAWRENCE

I have a drink for you.

WILSON

Oh, thank you!

LAWRENCE hands WILSON a drink.

LAWRENCE

Do you know Dr. Hibbard?

WILSON

Oh, yes, of course. How are you, Doctor?

CAMERA moves with MARY as she nears a large chair in which old MRS. LAWRENCE is seated.

MARY

Grandma Lawrence, can I get you something?

GRANDA LAWRENCE

Nothing more, I'm fine, thank you.

MARY passes a MALE GUEST, whose back is to us.

GUEST

Where's Dr. Rankin?

MARY

He'll be here in just a few minutes.

MALE GUEST

I want to have a word with him about that clock.

MARY goes over to MR. LUNDSTRUM, who, standing, is addressing a couple of other GUESTS, including MRS. RAND, who are seated.

MRS. RAND

And what was that Frenchman's name?

(to MARY)

Oh, hello, dear.

MR. LUNDSTRUM

Landru. There may well be ten . . . or a dozen . . . graves out there in those woods.

MRS. RAND

The autopsy showed that the murder to be committed just three weeks ago.

MARY moves away from the group toward an ELDERLY MALE GUEST. She attempts to take his teacup.

MARY

Can I get you some?

MALE GUEST

No, thank you.

LAWRENCE approaches.

MARY

Jeff, can I get you another drink?

WILSON advances toward MARY. The door opens, and RANKIN enters.

DR. HIBBARD

What does Emerson say about crime? Oh, there's Rankin; he may know.

RANKIN advances into the room.

RANKIN
(to Mary)

Sorry to be late.

HIBBARD

Oh, hello there, Rankin. Do you know that quote? "Commit a crime, and the earth is made of glass."

RANKIN

No, I don't.

WILSON
(quoting)

"Commit a crime, and the earth is made of glass. Commit a crime, and it seems as if a coat of snow fell on the ground, such as reveals in the woods the track of every partridge and fox and squirrel and mole. You cannot recall the spoken word, you cannot wipe out the foot-track, you cannot draw up the ladder, so as to leave no inlet or clew."

MRS. LAWRENCE approaches.

MRS. LAWRENCE

You're Mr. Wilson, aren't you? D'you know you are the number one suspect in our murder case?

WILSON

Oh?

MRS. LAWRENCE

So far, you're the only suspect. Potter put the finger on you. He thinks you committed the crime to get possession of some priceless antique.

RANKIN takes MARY by the arm, indicating that they should go elsewhere. As they pass through the crowd, they hear the voice of a FEMALE GUEST:

THE VOICE OF A FEMALE GUEST

Charles Rankin . . . I wish you'd left that clock alone.
Harper was a nice quiet place until it started banging.

MARY and RANKIN go into another room.

RANKIN

Mary, what's Wilson doing here?

MARY

I don't know.

RANKIN

You invited him, didn't you? What's he up to?

MARY

I don't know.

RANKIN

Are you all right?

MARY

Yes, quite all right.

DISSOLVE TO:
INT. HALLWAY—LATE AFTERNOON

MARY, RANKIN at her elbow, stands in the doorway, speeds
the last guests.

MARY

Good night!

She closes the door and turns, hard and composed. As she faces RANKIN, their eyes meet and hold. Her hand goes to her throat, and she runs one finger around the inside of the pearl necklace she is wearing, as though it were suddenly too tight for her.

RANKIN

Can I help you, dear?

He takes a step towards her. Then she raises both hands and attempts to unfasten the necklace. The catch sticks. She jerks at it. It still sticks.

MARY

No!

The string breaks, and the pearls fall. MARY suddenly breaks into a wild sobbing.

MARY

No! No!

SARA enters and watches them apprehensively.

RANKIN

Mary, Mary, Mary. It's all right, it's all right.

DISSOLVE TO:
INT. JUDGE LONGSTREET'S STUDY—
NIGHT

JUDGE LONGSTREET, NOAH, DR. LAWRENCE, and SARA are present with WILSON, to whom SARA is speaking. All eyes are fixed on her. She is sobbing.

SARA

It broke, and the beads fell all over the floor. He took her upstairs. When I left, I could still hear her crying.

WILSON

The floodgates have opened. Her subconscious has almost won.

(pause)

From now on, we must know every move Mrs. Rankin makes. She's never to leave the house, unless I know where she's going. If, for any reason, I can't be found . . . she's to be detained . . . no matter on what pretext. Do you understand, Sara?

JUDGE LONGSTREET
(his voice tortured)

When she snapped those beads, she signed her death warrant. We're carrying her life in our hands. Every time she walks on a slippery sidewalk . . . is near somehing that can fall . . . drives an automobile . . . anything that could result in accidental death . . . her life is in danger.

SARA
(grimly)

Don't worry. She won't get by me.

DISSOLVE TO:
INT. BELFRY—NIGHT

A thin wedge of moonlight stabs down from above onto the foot of the ladder. RANKIN is near the top, sawing through one of the rungs.

Outside, the clock in the tower strikes midnight. The mechanical angel passes in front of its face.

INT. WILSON'S ROOM—NIGHT

WILSON, in pajamas and dressing gown, stands at the window, smoking his pipe. The striking of the hour continues.

EXT. TOWN SQUARE—NIGHT

Through the window, WILSON sees the clock, the angel making his march as the hour chimes.

INT. MARY'S BEDROOM—NIGHT

The chiming of the clock has not ceased.

MARY lies in bed, moving around uneasily. She brings her hand to her forehead, then turns and goes back to sleep.

DISSOLVE TO:
INT. BELFRY—NIGHT

From the bottom of the ladder, we see RANKIN at the top, sawing.

INSERT: TIMETABLE ON RANKIN'S DESK. It reads:

3:25 PHONE MARY
3:30 Go to POTTER'S DRUG STORE
ESTABLISH TIME
4:00 LEAVE POTTER'S
Rankin's hand adds the last entry:
4:05 HOME

In a Harper classroom, OVER SCENE, there is the sound of footsteps and boys' voices as the class assembles. CAMERA PULLS BACK to FULL SHOT as RANKIN, rising from his desk, slips the paper into his pocket and faces the class. The wall clock indicates half past two. RANKIN's manner is relaxed. All strain has fallen from him.

RANKIN

Good afternoon, gentlemen.

BOYS

Good afternoon, sir.

RANKIN

(glancing at clock on wall behind him,
comparing it with his watch)

Today we will attempt to finish with the career of Friedrich der Grosse, König von Preussen, Kurfurst von Brandenberg, Prinz von Polen . . . Frederick the Great, to you . . .

DISSOLVE TO:
INT. POTTER'S DRUG STORE—DAY

RANKIN is in a phone booth. He puts a coin into the phone and dials. There is a sign that says, "Gentlemen, do not deface walls! Use pad for your convenience." Below is a notepad of paper, on which he draws a swastika as the phone rings.

In her house, MARY answers the phone.

MARY

Hello?

Back at the phone booth, RANKIN crosses out the swastika.

RANKIN

Mary, this is Charles. Can you hear me, dear? I can't speak very loud where I am, but I want you to understand this . . . something very important has come up. You must come to the church immediately. The church tower. You understand?

MARY

(on the phone)

Yes, I understand.

CHARLES

I don't want anybody to know that you're going there. Mary, don't tell anybody you're going. Go to the church. Leave your car in the rear, and come in through the back door. OK. Bye.

He hangs up and pulls open the door to the booth, tearing off the paper with the crossed-out swastika. As he does so, we hear POTTER's voice.

POTTER'S VOICE

Peabody!

PEABODY'S VOICE

I'm coming! I'm coming!

PEABODY comes in, carrying a load of firewood.

POTTER

Put that back there along with the rest of 'em, then get back to work.

PEABODY

Yes, sir.

RANKIN seats himself in the checker player's chair. POTTER
is already on his comfortable throne. PEABODY lets the load
of firewood tumble noisily down.

MR. POTTER

Watch that, Mr. Peabody . . . Your move, perfessor.

INT. RANKIN HOME

MARY, hatted and gloved, is coming down the stairs. She sits
down to put on her shoes. SARA appears at the living room
door, broom in hand.

SARA

Goin' someplace? Where to?

> *(Mary pretends not to hear
> the question. Starts on)*

I asked you where you were goin', Miss Mary.

MARY

(stops)

I heard.

SARA

Well?

MARY

Sara, you seem to forget, I'm not a child any longer but
a married woman.

SARA

You ain't been married very long . . .

MARY glances at her, surprised. Then decides to ignore SARA's
behavior, starts on.

SARA

Wait, Mrs. Rankin.

MARY
(sharply)

What is it? I'm in a hurry.

MARY has opened the door to leave.

SARA
(aggrieved)

Well, you don't need to go bitin' my head off.

MARY slams the door shut.

MARY

What is it, Sara?

SARA sobs. MARY grabs hold of her.

MARY

If you've got something to say, say it. What is it?

SARA

I don't know what's got into you lately, indeed I don't.
You was never mean to me like this, back at the old
house.

MARY
(resignedly)

Sara. . .

SARA

(raises the corner of her apron,
dabs at her eyes)

Maybe I've outworn my usefulness. I know I ain't as young as I used to be. Maybe you don't want me around anymore.

MARY

In heaven's name, stop talking such nonsense.

SARA

Well, it's true, and you know it. I'm going to pack my things and leave here, indeed I am.

SARA sits down, sobbing.

MARY

Sara, I'm sorry if I hurt your feelings. I didn't mean to, really I didn't. Sara, now I couldn't get along without you, and you know that, don't you? Well, don't you?

SARA

(through her tears)

Honestly?

MARY

(crossing her heart)

Honestly, honestly. You shan't ever leave me, Sara.

SARA clutches MARY to her, still sobbing.

SARA

You know the way I feel about you, like you was my own daughter, my own little girl.

MARY hugs her. Kisses her on the cheek.

MARY

Sara, I've got to go. I promised to be somewhere.

SARA

Where to, Miss Mary?

MARY

Stop fussing, Sara.

(smiling)

It's a secret.

MARY is at the front door, which she opens. SARA collapses. MARY rushes over.

SARA

Oh, Miss Mary!

MARY

What's the matter, Sara?

SARA

(gasping)

My heart . . . I can't breathe . . . the pain . . .

MARY puts a cushion under SARA's head.

MARY

Lie flat and keep quiet. Don't stir.

SARA obeys.

SARA

Don't leave me, Miss Mary. Maybe I'm dying.

MARY

No . . . I won't leave you.

She runs to the telephone, picks it up.

SARA

Stay with me!

MARY
(into the phone)

One three O, please . . .

NOAH answers the phone in the Longstreet house.

(after a pause)

MARY

Hello, Noah . . . I was supposed to meet Charles in the clock tower, but I can't get there. Will you go there and tell him to please wait for me? And, Noah . . . no one's to know where or why you're going or why. Ir's important.

NOAH

All right.

He hangs up the phone, troubled. Then he picks it up again.

NOAH
(into the phone)

Two three eight, please. Hello, may I speak to Mr. Wilson?

DISSOLVE TO:
INT. POTTER'S DAY

RANKIN and POTTER are sitting at the checkerboard.

POTTER

Looks like it's coming up for snow.

RANKIN makes a move and jumps several of POTTER's men. POTTER glares at RANKIN, determined to vanquish him.

We then see NOAH and WILSON walking briskly outside toward the church.

Mrs. RAND and Mrs. LUNDSTRUM come into the drugstore. RANKIN turns to greet the ladies.

RANKIN

Mrs. Rand . . . Mrs. Lundstrum . . . Isn't it after hours? You ladies are working too hard at the library . . .

MRS. LUNDSTRUM

Why, no, Mr. Rankin. We closed at 3:30 . . . as per usual.

RANKIN

You're perfectly right . . . I dismissed class 10 minutes early

(glances at the clock in the tower)

Three forty-four . . .

TRAVELING SHOT

As he speaks, the CAMERA begins to move slowly toward the window. We glimpse RANKIN, speaking to the ladies, as CAMERA CONTINUES TO MOVE until it seems to press against the pane. Across from Potter's we see NOAH and WILSON climbing the church steps.

RANKIN

. . . I've been playing checkers all this time with Mr. Potter and I didn't realize it.

MRS. RAND

You know what you are, Mr. Rankin? You're the absent-minded professor . . .

This bit of wit convulses her: she is in a state of mild hysteria as she and MRS. LUNDGARD move off and sit down at a nearby table.

DISSOLVE TO:
INT. BELFRY—AFTERNOON

The camera looks down from the belfry to the foot of the ladder. WILSON has begun climbing, followed by NOAH. The camera focuses on his hands as they grasp the rungs of the ladder. Finally WILSON's hand grasps one of the rungs RANKIN has sabotaged and then the other. The rungs snap, leaving WILSON dangling in midair.

Back at the drugstore, POTTER and RANKIN are still playing checkers.

POTTER

You sure are lucky today.

RANKIN

I am?

POTTER

You sure are.

VOICE OF MR. HILL

Evening, Mr. Potter.

POTTER

Evening, Mr. Hill.

VOICE OF HILL

Mr. Potter, I can't find them! The earmuffs!

POTTER

Right over there by the mittens!

(to RANKIN)

Be right back.

POTTER leaves the checkerboard.

RANKIN looks at his note, which says, "4:00 leave Potter's. 4:05 home."

POTTER
(off camera)

Right there in that box, where I told you they was.

VOICE OF MR. HILL

How much you want for them?

POTTER

Eighty-five cents.

VOICE OF MR. HILL

That's an awful lot!

POTTER

They come high this year.

POTTER comes back to the checkerboard and picks up a piece of crumpled-up paper. He sees RANKIN's note.

POTTER

You want this thing?

RANKIN

I'll keep it.

POTTER throws his own trash in the pot-bellied stove.

RANKIN

You know, Mr. Potter, you're a bad influence. I intended only to stay a couple of minutes; you've made me stay the whole afternoon. Look what time it is!

POTTER

I'd like to get even.

RANKIN

Your move.

Back at the church, WILSON is climbing down the bottom of the stairs. NOAH is already down.

WILSON

He really had the wind up. You can still smell the glue where he joined it.

INT. POTTER'S—DAY

POTTER and RANKIN are still playing checkers. They look out the window.

POTTER

It's like I told you, Professor. It's like we're coming up for snow.

RANKIN gets up and goes to the stove. He puts his own note into the stove, makes sure that it is burning, and throws it in.

POTTER makes a move that he thinks is brilliant.

POTTER

Look here, Professor. Double or nothing?

Without sitting back down, RANKIN makes a couple of moves on the checkerboard. He makes to leave.

RANKIN

Good afternoon, Mr. Potter.

POTTER

Afternoon, Mr. Rankin.

We now see the clock in the tower striking 4.

Light, feathery snow is now falling fast outside POTTER's window. RANKIN is walking outdoors.

At the RANKIN house, RANKIN comes in and closes the door. We see the silhouetted shadow of MARY in the background.

MARY

Charles?

RANKIN looks around him, startled and furious. He sees her and advances toward her in the living room.

RANKIN

You didn't go to the church?

MARY

Sara . . .

RANKIN

Sara? What about Sara?

MARY

Just as I was leaving, Sara had some kind of an attack. She's resting. Jeff said it wasn't very serious, but said I should stay with her.

RANKIN

Mm-hm.

RANKIN turns and distractedly begins to wind a grandfather clock.

MARY
(coming forward)

What's the matter, Charles?

RANKIN
(sharply)

Nothing's the matter.

MARY

Then why did you want me to go to the church? You said it was important!

RANKIN

Nothing's important, nothing actually. It's my sense of proportion, failing me these days.

MARY grasps him by the shoulders from behind.

MARY

Please, Charles, what is it?

RANKIN starts and slams the door of the grandfather clock.
MARY recoils.

RANKIN

I'm sorry. I've just begun to feel the strain.

(He smiles, trying for the old charm)

You see, I have my weak moments too. I'll tell you in my
own good time.

MARY

(tonelessly)

Have they found out anything more?

RANKIN

No, nothing. There's nothing to find out. Unless you . . .

MARY

No, I haven't seen anybody all day. I've been in my room.

RANKIN sits down.

RANKIN

(his self-control restored)

There's a rumor going around that there's an arrest to
be made.

*(rubs his right temple
with the heel of his hand)*

My head . . . The incident of the beads, yesterday, it made
me doubt your strength. I thought perhaps you'd gone
to your father and told him something. If you had . . .

MARY

You didn't have to be afraid . . . What did you tell Noah?

RANKIN

(without turning)

Mm. What—what about?

MARY

(looking up quickly)

Didn't you see him?

RANKIN

(not knowing what she is talking about)

Why should I have seen him?

MARY

Did you come here directly from the church?

RANKIN

(turning to her)

Am I being cross-examined?

MARY

No, but when I found I couldn't leave Sara, I called Noah
and told him to go there and tell you I was detained.

RANKIN

(furiously)

I told you not to call anybody.

MARY

But surely Noah . . .

RANKIN

(imperiously)

Call him and tell him not to go.

MARY

I can't. I talked to him over half an hour ago.

RANKIN

(suddenly shouting)

Call him, I say!

MARY

(all control gone)

He's gone!

RANKIN

If he dies, his blood will be on your hands.

MARY

(coming to her feet)

What are you saying . . .

RANKIN

(ranting)

It's your meddling that's done this. It would have been all right if it hadn't been for you. But you had to be here . . . on that day . . . hanging your stupid curtains . . . Calling Noah! . . .

MARY

(sharply)

Charles . . . have you killed Noah?

RANKIN

Yes, if he goes to the church and climbs up that ladder!

MARY

It was I you intented to kill.

• 114 •

RANKIN

No!

MARY

Why wasn't it I? Franz Kindler!

At the mention of his name, all expression leaves RANKIN's face. His eyes are dull, his mouth hanging slightly open.

MARY

Kill me. Kill me. I want you to. I couldn't face life knowing what I've been to you . . . and what I've done to Noah. When you kill me, don't put your hands on me. Here . . . use this . . .

She picks up a poker and holds it out to him.

EXT. RANKIN HOUSE—DAY

JUDGE LONGSTREET drives his big sedan towards the house at high speed. In it are WILSON, DR. LAWRENCE, and NOAH. The car skids to a stop in front of the house.

INT. RANKIN LIVING ROOM—
AFTERNOON

Close-up of the poker being thrown to the floor.

The men rush into the RANKIN house. A door is swinging, indicating that RANKIN has fled. MARY stands dazed while NOAH comes up to her.

NOAH

Mary!

MARY

Oh!

MARY faints into NOAH's arms. From her point of view, we see NOAH's face close up and blurred as we hear WILSON on the phone.

WILSON

(tapping on the phone)

Operator? Operator! Get me the state police!

We see the clock in the tower striking ominously.

WILSON

(on the phone)

Yes . . . the roadblocks are up. We're watching the railroad station, and he isn't hiding in the woods . . .

MARY is lying in her bed in her room. She comes to full awakening. She gets up; we see her through the mirror in her nightgown. She picks up her coat, puts it on, and leaves.

Outside, we see her walking from her house.

In MARY's bedroom, SARA looks in to find her missing.

SARA

Judge Longstreet! Judge Longstreet!

We see MARY walking through a cemetery in the snow.

The men rush outside of RANKIN's house.

JUDGE LONGSTREET

Get Wilson, Noah! I'll go for the police!

JUDGE LONGSTREET and NOAH run off in different directions.

Outside the church, MARY walks in through the back door.

NOAH rushes into the RANKIN living room, where WILSON is still on the phone.

NOAH

Mr. Wilson!

WILSON

If he's where I think he is, it's going to be easy. We'll do everything possible to get him alive.

NOAH

She's gone, Mr. Wilson! She's not in the house!

WILSON
(throws the receiver on the hook
and turns to Noah, his voice quiet
but his eyes full of anxiety)

The clock tower?

NOAH

I don't know.

WILSON
(grimly)

If that's where he's hiding, and she gets there before us . . .

NOAH
(in a small voice)

What will we do?

WILSON
(rushing out of the room,
shouting after him)

Call Captain Samuels, and the deputies! Get all the help you can!

NOAH

Where?

WILSON takes a fall on the stairs and cries out in pain. NOAH reacts and dashes down the stairway toward him.

NOAH

Mr. Wilson!

With NOAH helping him, WILSON gets painfully to his feet.

WILSON
(gasping through his teeth)

The church . . . the church . . .

NOAH

But what about you, Mr. Wilson?

WILSON
(breathing hard as he starts to move)

Hurry up now! While your sister may be still alive!

With a worried look at WILSON, NOAH hurries off scene. WILSON hobbles after him.

WILSON
(grimly)

I'll get there . . .

DISSOLVE TO:
INT. VESTIBULE—NIGHT

MARY, a package under her arm, begins mounting towards the belfry. She sees the ladder with its missing section. Clutching a package under one arm, with her free hand she grasps the one still standing upright and mounts up to the top.

RANKIN'S VOICE comes out of the darkness.

RANKIN'S VOICE

Don't move. I have a gun.

CLOSE SHOT—MARY

She stands rigid on the ladder.

MARY
(quietly)

You don't need it. I'm alone.

RANKIN (incredulously)

What are you doing here?

MARY
Lift me up. (levelly)

RANKIN hoists her up.

RANKIN

You're telling the truth?

MARY

Why should I lie?

RANKIN

Were you followed here?

MARY

I came by our way. Through the cemetery. No one saw me.

INT. BELFRY—NIGHT
INT. LANDING—NIGHT

RANKIN throws open the door to the clock room, and he and MARY go in. She still carries her package. Silently, she hands him the package. She watches him as he tears the paper, revealing a shoebox. He jerks off the lid. He is staring down at emptiness. He looks up at her slowly.

MARY
(quietly)

I needed the excuse. I was afraid you wouldn't let me up.

RANKIN

What do you want?

MARY

I came to kill you.

RANKIN

No, Mary, it's you that are going to die. You were meant to fall through that ladder. You're going to fall.

MARY

I don't mind. If I take you with me.

RANKIN

You are a fool. They've searched the woods. I watched them like God looking at little ants . . . They've sure they've done such a fine search they won't search it again. A day or two and they'll be sure I've gotten out of town.

MARY

Not when they find me. They'll know you're still here.

RANKIN

But darling, you're on the verge of a breakdown. Now, you've cracked. Why else would you leave your bed . . . come to an empty church tower in the dead of night . . . ? Any child could see you'd wind up killing yourself.

He is interrupted by the sudden slamming of the clock tower door. WILSON stands before him. RANKIN draws a gun out of his pocket.

WILSON

(sweating with pain,
but his tone cool and final)

Killing is what led you here. It won't help you now.

RANKIN draws the gun on WILSON. MARY grabs at RANKIN's arm for it. He pushes her aside and lunges for WILSON.

WILSON

Look out the window! Look!

RANKIN

That's on old trick, Wilson! And a very poor trick!

WILSON

Tricks! That's all you know is tricks! I don't need any tricks! No matter what happens to me, tricks won't do you any good! You're finished, Herr Franz Kindler!

VOICES are heard. We see a crowd of CITIZENS rushing toward the church. RANKIN looks through a window, sees them, is alarmed.

WILSON

The citizens of Harper. They've come after you. The plain little ordinary people, the ones you've been laughing at, have friends, Franz Kindler. Well, you can't fool them anymore.

RANKIN rushes toward WILSON but halts.

WILSON

Oh, sure, you can kill me . . . Mary . . . half of the people down there. There's no escape. You had a world and it closed in on you till there was only Harper. That closed in on you and there was only this room. And this room, too, is closing in on you. . .

RANKIN's face has again been stripped of all expression; the eyes are dull, the mouth hanging open. As WILSON's indictment sinks into him, a faint moistness appears on his lips. His eyes come alive, crazed, frenetic. Suddenly he is slobbering.

RANKIN

It's not true, the things they said I did. It was not my idea. I followed orders.

WILSON

You gave the orders.

RANKIN

I only did my duty.

(pleading)

Don't send me back. I can't face them. I'm not a criminal.

MARY

You *are.*

RANKIN turns to face her. This is the moment WILSON has waited for. He strikes out at RANKIN's wrist. The gun flies across the room. It lands at MARY's feet. She snatches it up. Her hand is steady as she faces him.

RANKIN rushes up the belfry, into the works of the clock, which he causes to go haywire. From below, MARY fires at RANKIN, hitting him in the arm. RANKIN falls onto a platform.

WILSON

Give me that gun!

WILSON takes the gun from MARY and fires, but it is empty. RANKIN rushes out to the window ledge and plunges out. He falls onto the outside platform of the clock, where the angel and devil are moving. He makes his way past the devil, but the outstretched sword in the hand of the angel skewers RANKIN. When it stops moving, he frees himself and pushes the angel down on the CROWD, who flee back. The clockworks go haywire, the hands rushing wildly around the dial. RANKIN falls to the ground. The crowd is screaming. The clock's hands swing round and round furiously.

The scene turns to the interior of the church. We, and WILSON, are looking down at the CROWD. MARY is descending the ladder and reaches the bottom. POTTER is at the foot of the stairs.

POTTER

OK, let me give you a hand, Mr. Wilson!

WILSON

No, no, no, thanks!

POTTER

What happened?

WILSON

V-E Day in Harper.

POTTER

I don't get that. Come on down!

WILSON

No, no. Not until you get me a new ladder. I've had my ankle busted and my head conked. From here on in, I'm taking it easy!

POTTER

Well, I'll get you another ladder, Mr. Wilson. You've had enough trouble.

MARY looks up at WILSON, who is puffing on his pipe.

WILSON

Good night, Mary. Pleasant dreams.

FADE OUT:

THE END

ABOUT THE FILM

The Stranger (1946), the third film directed by the legendary Orson Welles, is a film noir thriller of the highest order.

In the wake of World War II, Mr. Wilson, an official with the Allied War Crimes Commission (played by the legendary Edward G. Robinson), is on the trail of Franz Kindler, an escaped Nazi who was the chief architect of the regime's mass genocide. Wilson allows a concentration camp commandant, Conrad Meinike, to escape in the hope that he will lead him to the elusive Kindler. The trail takes them to the quiet Connecticut town of Harper, where Kindler (played by Welles) has taken on the guise of Charles Rankin, a history teacher at a boys' school.

Kindler, as Rankin, is about to marry Mary Longstreet (Loretta Young), the daughter of an eminent Supreme Court justice, Adam Longstreet (Philip Merivale). Wilson has to establish Rankin's identity as Kindler and overcome Mary's disbelief.

The drama centers around a Gothic clock in a church at the center of Harper, which has not worked for many years. Rankin undertakes to restore the clock—thereby providing a clue to his identity with the Nazi Kindler, who has a mania for clocks.

The Stranger has the plot and pacing of a thriller, contrasting the profound evil of Kindler and Meinike with the naivete of a small New England town. Its sharp characterizations include the relentless Wilson, the suave Rankin, the earnest and devoted Mary, her loyal and vigilant brother Noah (played by Richard Long), and the grave but affectionate Judge Longstreet.

In an attempt to convince Mary of Rankin's true identity, Wilson shows her then-recent newsreel footage of the Holocaust. The Stranger is the first Hollywood film to show this shocking but authentic footage.

In addition to the dramatic and tightly paced story, *The Stranger* features many characteristics of Welles' masterful directorial hand: the use of shadows to create stark chiaroscuro effects; unusual and startling camera angles; and trailing camera shots that move individual scenes across locations.

The Stranger is a classic example of the Hollywood film noir genre. It will enthrall not only aficionados but anyone who appreciates the power of a compelling, tightly paced thriller.